dog · day
detectives

Silverleaf Press are available exclusively
through Independent Publishers Group.

For details write or telephone
Independent Publishers Group, 814 North Franklin St.
Chicago, IL 60610, (312) 337-0747

Silverleaf Press
8160 South Highland Drive
Sandy, Utah 84093

MINI-MYSTERIES
FOR A SUMMER DAY

By Rick Walton

Illustrated by
Rebecca Waddington

SILVERLEAF
PRESS

DRAGON

Someone has stolen a baby from the Zoo....

"Just imagine. The komodo dragon grows up to ten feet long and can eat eighty percent of its weight at one meal!" Sarah Arthur said as she stared at the world's largest lizard, housed safely behind glass in the Reptile House at the Paris Fork Zoo.

"Cool!" said her brother Nicholas. He had read the sign a hundred times, but still thought the fact was fascinating. "How much do you weigh? I'll bet the Komodo could eat you and Gator together." Gator looked up from nibbling on Nicholas's shoelaces and barked.

"Don't worry, boy," Nicholas said. "We won't feed you to the dragon . . . unless you untie my shoelaces again."

Sarah moved on, and looked into a smaller habitat. "There's supposed to be a baby in here, but I don't see it. They keep the babies separate because the grownups eat them."

"That's rude," Nicholas said. "I'd be very upset if our parents wanted to eat us. Is the baby behind that tree or hiding behind a rock?"

"I don't think so. The babies are born a foot long, so they can't hide very easily."

Sarah noticed a passing zoo docent. "Excuse me," she said. "Do you know where the baby Komodo is?"

"We wish we knew," the lady said. "He disappeared some time this morning, not long ago. It's possible, though not likely, that he escaped on his own. It's more likely that someone stole him."

"Stole him!" said Sarah. "Why would someone do that? Aren't Komodos dangerous?"

"Watch out, Gator," Nicholas said to the dog, who was now sniffing the docent's shoes.

"They're very dangerous," said the docent. "Especially when they're full grown. And it's not just their teeth that you have to worry about. Their saliva is full of deadly bacteria. But Komodos sell for a lot of money on the black market. They. . . ."

The docent was interrupted by three men who walked up to the baby Komodo habitat. One was a security guard, one a middle-aged man who looked like he was a zoo official, and one was a young man, probably around twenty.

The zoo official smiled. "Nicholas! Sarah!" He looked down. "Gator! It's always good to see you guys here!"

"Hi Dave," Sarah said.

"Uh, Mr. Garrick," the security guard said. "I thought dogs weren't allowed in the zoo?"

"They're generally not," said Dave Garrick. "But Gator's a special dog. Ever since he caught the flamingo thief last year we let him in. Besides," he smiled, "Nicholas and Sarah's dad is the manager of the Paris Fork Arts and Recreation Council. He's kind of our boss."

The security guard reached down and patted Gator. "In that case, boy, tell my boss I deserve a raise."

"Okay now, show us," said Dave, turning to the young man they had come in with. "How exactly did you get that Komodo out?"

"Did they find it?" the docent asked.

Dave said, "They did, thank goodness. And it's just fine. This young man was carrying it out the front gate in a cooler. The guard here heard a scratching sound coming from the cooler and investigated. This boy says he stole it by himself, but he hasn't been able to explain to us to our satisfaction how he did it. There are doors and locks. You can't just walk into the zoo and pick up an expensive, dangerous lizard."

"But I did," said the young man. "Here, I'll show you." He took off his jacket and laid it on a nearby bench. Gator raced over to investigate. The young man continued, "I climbed over the bar. . . ."

"There's no bar here," said Nicholas. "You're thinking of the Lion House. You didn't steal a lion too, did you? I want to see it."

"No, uh . . . okay. There's a door somewhere around here. I went in that and found that lizard's door and I took the lizard because I thought he was cute. I was just going to take him to show my mom and then I was going to bring him back."

Just then a fourth man came up. "Hi Bob," said the docent.

"What's up?" Bob said.

"Hey, Bob," said Dave. "You fed the Komodos about an hour ago, didn't you? Was the baby there? Did you see anything unusual? Did you see this guy lurking around?"

"The baby was there, all right. He snapped at me. Besides that, nothing unusual. And I've never seen this guy before in my life."

"You locked the doors?" Sarah asked. "Didn't forget and leave something open?"

"Who are you, kid? Shirley-Lock Holmes?" Bob said. He laughed and turned back to Mr. Garrick "I know what would happen if a Komodo got out. I'm always sure to lock everything when I leave."

"Any idea how this guy could have stolen a baby Komodo?"

"He stole a Komodo?" said Bob. "This guy's nuts."

"Guess we'd better call the police," said Dave. "Maybe they can get this guy to explain how he did it." The guard grabbed the young man's arm and they began to walk away.

"Hey, don't forget your jacket, kid," Bob said. Dave reached for the jacket. He had to wrestle it away from Gator, and when Gator finally let go, Dave handed it to the culprit. "And let me know what they find out, "Bob said. "I wanna know how he got that Komodo so we can keep it from happening again."

"Uh, gentlemen, an announcement, please," Nicholas stared up at the men. "I know how that guy got the baby Komodo out."

How did the young man get the Komodo dragon, and how did Nicholas know? (Answer on p. 137.)

WHAT A BITE!

Is Gator really a ferocious, biting beast?

"Is this your dog?" The man at the door looked serious. He had Gator by the collar and was holding him tight.

"You let go of my dog," said Sarah, who had answered the door.

"So it *is* your dog," said the man. "Then I guess I get to sue you."

"What's this about suing?" said Mr. Arthur who had come up behind Sarah. The entire Arthur family was soon there.

"Your dog bit me! And I plan to sue. Though maybe we can settle out of court. I'll need my medical bills paid for, and something to cover my emotional distress."

"Now, now," said Mr. Arthur, "let's just talk this over

calmly. Tell me what happened. Won't you come in?"

"I'll just stay out here," said the man.

"Let go of Gator!" said Sarah. Gator was pulling, trying to get away from the man's grasp.

"I think I'll just keep hold of him, thank you," said the man. "I don't want him to bite me again."

"Okay, okay," said Mr. Arthur. "Please, just tell me what happened."

"This dog bit me!"

"Yes," said Mr. Arthur. "You said that. Tell us what happened. When did it happen? How did it happen?"

"I was walking down the sidewalk in front of your house when this beast," he tugged on Gator's collar, "jumped out of the bushes and bit me!"

"Gator would never bite anyone," said Sarah. "Unless they deserved it. What did you do to him? I'll bet you were kicking him. Gator, was he kicking you?"

"Yip!" said Gator.

"I wasn't kicking him. I didn't even see him until he jumped out of the bushes and bit me."

"When did this happen?" asked Mr. Arthur.

"Yesterday. He bit me yesterday."

"You're lying! Dad, he's lying."

"I'm not lying. That dog bit me yesterday."

"If he bit you yesterday," said Mr. Arthur, "why didn't you talk to us right then?"

"Well, duh," said the man. "I'd just been bitten by a dog! And how was I to know if he was rabid or not. I called an ambulance on my cell phone and had them take me to the hospital. I got stitches."

"Liar!" said Sarah.

"Sarah!" said Mr. Arthur. "We don't talk like that to guests."

"Sorry, Dad," said Sarah. "But he's a liar! I'll bet he didn't even have any stitches. I'll bet he just made the whole thing up."

"I did not make the whole thing up!" said the man and he pulled up his pant leg. "See!"

He pointed to a large, light-brown scar on his leg. "That's where he bit me! He gave me that scar!"

The man pulled his pant leg back down. He calmed down some, and then said, "I don't want to make this any worse than it already is. If you just settle up with me, we could call this case closed, and we won't have to meet in court."

"How much do you need to settle this case?" said Mr. Arthur.

"I think zero cents is about right," said Nicholas. "Now you'd better let Gator go right now and then get out of here, or we will see you in court—as a defendant in a fraud case!"

"Now wait a minute," said the man. "How dare you talk to me like that!"

"I dare because I know Gator never bit you," said Nicholas. "And I can prove it!"

What did Nicholas know? (Answer on p. 137.)

WEST SIDE STORY

Difficult directions and a missing building.

Gator couldn't jump high enough to catch the frisbee, so when Nicholas threw it, Gator would chase after it and pick it up and bring it back. "Jump, Gator!" Nicholas would say. But Gator would just watch the frisbee land, and then he'd get it.

"Okay, so my dog isn't a jumping dog," Sarah said. "But he's a smart dog, and that's better."

The kids were playing at Pioneer Park. It was a safe park, with lots of parents with young kids and lots of space. There were modern playgrounds, a Pioneer Museum, a baseball diamond, and even a community pool with water slides.

But it was time to go.

"Come on, Gator," Sarah said. "Give Nicholas back his frisbee. It's time to go get Mom."

Their mother was a computer consultant. Today she was working for a company a few blocks away, a company the kids had never been to before. The company's name was New Vibes. They produced software that helped you meditate and relax. Mrs. Arthur had told the kids to meet her there at 5 p.m., and she would give them a ride home.

"Do you have the directions?" Sarah asked Nicholas.

"Right here," Nicholas said. He pulled a piece of paper out of his pocket and waved it in the air.

"Step one: go to the Fifth Avenue entrance to the park. That's this way." Nicholas pointed to the parking lot entrance.

At the entrance Nicholas looked at his paper again. "Step two: go east three blocks." Nicholas looked around. "The sun is setting to the right of us, so that's west. East is to the left."

The note could have just said, "Turn left," but Mrs. Arthur was trying to help the kids learn compass directions.

The kids and dog headed left.

After they had walked three blocks, they reached University Avenue. Gator turned right and started across the street, but Sarah stopped him. "No, Gator. We're not going to the Pizza Shoppe," she said. Gator loved pizza.

"Where next?" She asked Nicholas.

"Step three: go south two blocks. You'll see the New Vibes building on your left."

"This way," Nicholas said, and he headed left again.

After two blocks, the kids started looking for the New Vibes building, but they couldn't find it. There was a Pizza Hut, which Gator barked at while looking hopefully at Sarah, a bank, an Indian restaurant, a dry cleaner, but no New Vibes building.

"Maybe Mom was wrong about how far we were supposed to go," Sarah said. "Let's keep going a little ways, and maybe we'll find the building."

They walked for two more blocks, but no New Vibes building.

"Maybe she made a mistake," Nicholas said. Maybe it was supposed to be on the right side of the street."

The kids and Gator walked back the way they came, this time looking on the other side of the street.

No New Vibes building.

When they finally reached Fifth Avenue again, they stopped. And then Nicholas slapped his forehead and said, "Well, duh! I know where the building is!"

Where was the building? (Answer on p. 138.)

A BARGAIN

Are the old letters a prize exhibit or a scam?

"All we have to do now is make sure they're authentic," Mr. Arthur said at dinner. "And then we'll buy them for the historical museum. Cheap, if you ask me."

Mr. Arthur had come home from work excited. A stranger had come in off the street with a stack of letters from famous people when they were kids. He needed some money, and said that if the city bought them quickly, he would sell them for much less than they were worth.

"Letters from famous people after they became famous are pretty common," Mr. Arthur said. "But letters written when they were kids are quite rare."

"Of course they're rare," Sarah said. "Kids don't write letters. Only grown-ups do."

"Of course kids write letters," Mrs. Arthur said. "Remember last Christmas? You wrote thank-you letters to your grandparents. And you've been writing to your friend Abby since she moved away last year."

"I e-mail her," Sarah said.

"E-mail is letters," Mrs. Arthur said. "Besides, a long time ago letter writing was an art, and children were encouraged to write letters."

"Did he say where he got them?" Nicholas asked.

"Apparently, from what he said, his great-grandfather knew their parents," Mr. Arthur said. "He would give the kids gifts, and they would write him thank you letters and tell him what was going on in their lives."

"So when will you know whether they're real or not?" Sarah asked.

"I'm going to call an expert tomorrow," Mr. Arthur said. "We'll have to fly him in, it will be expensive, but if they're authentic, it will be well worth it."

"I'd love to see them," Nicholas said.

"You'll be able to when they're in the museum," Sarah said.

"Oh, he can see them right now," Mr. Arthur said. He got up and went over to a table where his briefcase was. He reached in and pulled out a file folder. "Come into the living room. We probably shouldn't look at these near the food."

The rest of the Arthur family jumped up and followed Mr. Arthur into the living room. Mr. Arthur sat on the sofa, and spread the letters out on the coffee table. "Make sure your hands are clean and dry," he said. "And be very careful. These are valuable letters. And you, Gator," Mr. Arthur smiled, "keep your grubby paws off these papers."

"Arf!" Gator wagged his tail and grinned a big doggie grin.

Nicholas sat down next to Mr. Arthur and began to look through the letters.

They looked old. The paper was worn, slightly browning at the edges. The ink looked like they came from fountain pens, the old kind, and not from modern ballpoint pens.

Nicholas read through some of the letters. They sounded like letters that kids would write, even smart kids who would grow up to be famous. They talked about the presents they'd received, and what they were doing, and what was going on with their families.

Nicholas also admired the handwriting. Kids long ago obviously spent more time learning to write well. They're cursive was clean and readable. Even their signatures were easy to read. And they were impressive signatures: Mark Twain, Lewis Carroll, Ben Franklin.

Gator had finally had enough of being left out.

He jumped up on Nicholas, grabbed one of the letters, and ran into the kitchen with it.

Mr. Arthur was shocked. "Gator! Stop that! You're ruining an expensive artifact!"

"Oh, I wouldn't worry Dad," Nicholas said. "I doubt it's worth anything. Since these letters aren't real."

How did Nicholas know the letters were fakes? (Answer on p. 138.)

PURPLE POND PARK

A perfect place for the Dog Days of Summer

It was hot. Man it was hot. And when it was hot most of the kids in the neighborhood went to Purple Pond Park. Purple Pond wasn't really purple, but it was surrounded by purple flowers.

And on a hot day it was also surrounded by kids cooling down, pets running around, and vendors selling ice cream and other snacks.

On this hot, hot summer day Nicholas and Sarah had decided to take Gator and Davy for a swim. Or rather, for a wade. Purple Pond was only about a foot deep. Not too deep to be much danger, but deep enough to get kids wet. That's why the city let kids play there.

Nicholas pumped up three inner tubes—a foot of water is plenty to float on. And Sarah grabbed the towels.

"I want to take my owls!" said Davy. He clutched four of them. Davy loved stuffed owls. He liked their big eyes, and he would talk to them like they were real. To him they were.

"You can't take your owls, Davy," said Sarah. "They'll get wet. You don't want your owls to get wet. They might catch cold."

"I won't let them get wet," said Davy. "They'll stay away from the water."

"You can't carry four owls all the way to the park," said Nicholas.

"Gator can carry one," said Davy.

"Arf," said Gator.

"Gator would eat it," said Nicholas.

"How about this, Davy," said Sarah. "Pick your best owl and take it. And then when you come home your owl can tell the other owls all about our day at the park."

Davy looked at his owls for a moment and said, "Okay." He put the owls down, looked over them carefully, and then picked his large white one. "I'll take this one," he said.

At the park the kids picked an open spot of grass in the sun and laid down their towels. Nicholas and Sarah put their tubes on their towels. Davy put his owl on the towel first. Then he covered it with his inner tube. "This way he won't get sunburned," Davy said.

"The dinosaurs are going to eat your owl," said Nicholas, pointing to Davy's tube, which was decorated with Tyrannosaurs.

"They'll protect him," said Davy.

The kids rushed to the pond and waded in. Gator jumped in after them. Davy pretended he was swimming. He really could swim, just not in one foot of water.

After getting good and wet, Sarah said, "Time for tube races! Last one back with their tube is a frog."

The three kids sloshed out of the pond and ran back to their tubes.

Davy stopped and gasped. "My tube! It's gone!"

"Looks like your owl ate the dinosaurs," said Nicholas.

Davy didn't answer. He was looking around.

Gator was looking too. At the owl. He sniffed it. He sniffed around it. And then he took off.

Davy raced after him, followed by Nicholas and Sarah. Gator led them to the other side of the park and began barking at a boy was sitting on an inner tube, a tube that looked just like Davy's.

"You took my tube!" said Davy.

"Arf!" said Gator. And then he growled.

"I did not," said the boy. "I got this tube for my birthday. My parents bought it for me."

"It's my tube!" said Davy. "It was sitting on my best owl. You probably want to steal it, too!"

"Why would I want to steal an owl?" said the boy.

"He may not want to steal an owl," said Nicholas, "but you definitely stole that tube from my little brother. And I can prove it. Now give it back or else I'll sic Gator on you. He's not named Gator for nothing."

"Arf!" said Gator.

How could Nicholas prove that the boy had stolen Davy's tube? (Answer on p. 138.)

GATOR AID

"Can't you slow that dog down?"

"I'm getting hungry," Sarah said as she tugged on Gator's leash, or rather, as he tugged on her. It was hard to keep up with Gator when he was on a walk.

"Me too," Nicholas said. He trotted along to keep up. "Can't you slow that dog down?"

"He's hungry too," Sarah said. "Gator, slow down!"

"Arf!" Gator barked, without slowing down.

The kids hurried along down the sidewalk, looking for some place to stop and eat. They'd spent the morning playing at a park and exploring downtown Paris Fork. They were planning to meet their dad at his office when he got off work, and he'd take them out to dinner. But that was a long way off. Fortunately their dad had given them some money for lunch.

"How about Mexican?" Nicholas said.

"We ate Mexican yesterday," Sarah said. "How about pizza?"

"Pizza's good," Nicholas said. "And Gator likes pizza."

Gator heard both his name and one of his favorite foods in the same phrase, and he turned and yipped.

They found a pizza place and bought a large barbecue chicken pizza to go. Sarah and Nicholas were starved, and would have liked to have just eaten there, but they knew that Gator's table manners weren't always appropriate for polite company. They'd have an easier time if they took the pizza to a park.

"Let me carry the pizza," Nicholas said to his sister, who balanced the pizza with one hand while tugging on Gator's leash with the other.

"I can do it," Sarah said. "Besides, this way I get to smell the pizza all the way to the park."

Gator turned around at the word "pizza" and barked again. This time he could smell the pizza too. But he smelled something else. And then he saw it. A squirrel. Gator barked and raced around Sarah. The leash jerked Sarah and spun her around. She barely held onto the pizza.

"Whoa, boy!" she shouted.

The squirrel saw Gator and raced across the street, almost getting hit by a truck. Gator turned and raced after him, but when he came to the end of the leash, he was jerked on his tail.

So was Sarah, whose legs were tangled in the leash. She fell on her side, barely keeping the pizza from sliding out of the box. "Ouch! Gator! Stop pulling! You're hurting me. And you're going to ruin our pizza. Hey, Nicholas. Don't just stand there, untangle me and hold onto Gator while I see if I broke anything."

"Here, let me help," said an older boy who had just arrived on the scene. He untangled the leash and handed it to Nicholas. "Now let's see where you're hurt," he said. "My dad's a doctor and I know a bit about broken bones." He picked up the pizza, smiled as he smelled it, and set it next to a lamp post.

When Gator saw him pick up the pizza, he started barking at him.

"Settle down, Gator," Sarah said. "He's just helping." She smiled up at the boy. She thought he was cute.

Gator settled into a low growl, but he didn't attack. He did watch carefully though.

"Come on, Sarah," Nicholas said. "You're okay. Let's get to the park and eat. I'm starving."

"Now just a minute," said the older boy. "She might be hurt, and moving her could make it worse." He looked her over, and then took her by the elbow. He lifted it up. "Does this hurt?"

"A little," said Sarah. "I think I scraped my elbow."

"You've done more than that," the boy said. "I'm pretty sure you broke your funny bone. I fractured mine once and there was nothing funny about it. I had my arm in a cast for a month."

He turned to Nicholas. "You, boy. . . ."

"My name's Nicholas," Nicholas said, a little annoyed. "My sister's okay. Get up Sarah, let's get going."

"Bad idea," said the boy. "You need to get her right away to the hospital. She might need a cast." He carefully helped Sarah to her feet. "Now, Nicholas, you hold on to her with both hands. Don't let her fall over again." He wrapped Nicholas's arms around Sarah and started leading them down the street.

Nicholas jerked his arms away. "You're a fraud and a thief," he said. "And you're not stealing our pizza! Now get lost before I sic our dog on you."

"GRRRRR!" Gator bared his teeth at the boy and then ran over to guard the pizza.

How did Nicholas know that the boy wasn't being honest with them? (Answer on p. 138.)

Happy Birthday To...
What Was That!?

Ellie's sleepover turns scary.

"Happy birthday, dear Ellie! Happy birthday to you!" the kids sang.

"Aroooo!" Gator joined in.

When the song was over, Ellie took a deep breath, and, in one quick burst of air, blew out all eight of her candles.

"The trick," said Ellie, "is to blow really hard and fast from right above the cake."

"I taught her that," said Joseph, her brother.

Ellie and Joseph Ivy were Sarah and Nicholas's cousins and best friends. They lived just a few blocks away and were the same ages. Sarah and Nicholas had been invited over for a birthday sleepover.

"Cut the cake! Cut the cake!" said Sarah.

"Scoop the ice cream! Scoop the ice cream!" said Nicholas.

"Arf! Arf!" said Gator.

"You'll all get plenty," said Uncle James, Joseph and Ellie's father, who took out a large knife and began to cut large slices. "And maybe there will be some leftovers for a midnight snack," he said slyly. He gave Nicholas a mischievous wink.

After cake and ice cream it was time for presents. Everyone helped clean up, and then they sat around the kitchen table. Ellie's mother, Aunt Jo, handed Ellie presents one by one. Sarah's present was a computer game that her mother had worked on. Nicholas gave her a book of puzzles. As Ellie opened her presents, everyone oohed and awed.

Finally there was just one present left. Aunt Jo handed the large box over to Ellie. "It's from your Grandma Ivy," said Aunt Jo. Ellie tore the wrapping off of the box and threw it in the corner of the kitchen where Gator jumped in it and started chewing.

Ellie opened the box. All she could see was bubble wrap. She started pulling it out and throwing it over to Gator. "Pop!"

"Gator," said Sarah, "stop chewing the bubble wrap!"

Ellie pulled out a carefully wrapped bundle. She

removed the tape and unwrapped it. It was a ceramic doll. "She's beautiful!" said Ellie.

"And she looks very fragile and very expensive," said Aunt Jo. "So be careful how you play with her."

The kids played some games, watched a video, and then it was time for bed. Because it was a special occasion, the kids got to sleep in the TV room—the girls on the couches, and the boys in sleeping bags on the floor. Gator slept on the floor next to Sarah's couch. The kids talked for a while, and then one by one drifted off.

"Grrrrrrr. . . ."

"What's that Gator?" said Sarah. "Do you hear something?"

"What is it?" asked Ellie.

"Gator growls like that when there's something wrong," said Nicholas.

"Looks like we're all awake now," said Joseph. "What's going on?"

"Gator hears something," said Sarah.

"Do you think it's a burglar?" said Ellie.

"Sure," said Joseph. "He's come to steal your birthday presents. No, it's probably just the wind. Or a mouse."

"Ewww!" said Ellie, and she curled up under her blanket. "I don't like mice. Especially at night."

"It's nothing," said Nicholas. "I'm going back to sleep."

"Me too," said Joseph.

"Grrrrrrrr. . . ." said Gator.

And then, "BANG BANG BANG BANG BANG!"

Gator started barking loudly, and then took off to investigate the noise.

"It is a burglar!" said Ellie. "And he's shooting!"

"We've got to hide," said Joseph.

"Go stop them, Nicholas! And help Gator! He's going to get hurt!" said Sarah.

"Are you crazy? I'm not going after a mad gunman, no matter what Gator did."

And then he stopped. And he laughed. "On the other hand. . . ." said Nicholas, and he climbed out of the sleeping bag and headed off in the direction of the gunfire.

"Stop, Nicholas!" said Sarah. "I didn't mean it. Go stop him, Joseph!"

"What?" said Joseph. "And me get shot too?"

"All right," said Sarah. "He's my brother." And she started to climb off the couch."

But as her feet touched the floor, Nicholas returned, biting a slice of cake. Behind him was Gator, his mouth covered with frosting. "It was just as I thought," Nicholas said.

What had Nicholas and Gator seen? (Answer on p. 139.)

STARRY STATES

Grandpa Arthur's Great Adventure

"It was back in 1949," Grandpa Arthur began. He was visiting his grandkids for the weekend. The kids loved listening to his stories, though they weren't always sure what parts to believe.

"It was long before your grandma caught my eye. I'd just graduated from high school and wanted an adventure. If I remember right, which I'm sure I do, I was 17 years old. About your age, Alan." Grandpa nodded and smiled at Nicholas and Sarah's oldest brother.

"Now don't you get any ideas," Mrs. Arthur said to Alan.

Grandpa continued. "I packed a few supplies, grabbed Gopher, my pup. . . ."

"Gator's grandpa?" Sarah asked.

"Yip?" Gator barked, curious.

43

"Gator's great-great-great-great . . . let me see . . . great-great—maybe a few more greats—Grandpa," said Grandpa. "Anyway, I kissed my parents and little sisters goodbye, promised to write, and off we went."

"Where'd you go, Grandpa?" said Sarah. "I hope somewhere fun, like Disneyland."

"Disneyland wasn't even built then," Nicholas said.

"Oh, I went somewhere much more fun than that," said Grandpa. "I visited every state in this country of ours. All 50 of them."

"That's a lot of walking, Dad," said Mr. Arthur.

"Sure was," said Grandpa. "Reckon I put in about 25,000 miles. Not all on foot, mind you. There was an occasional good Samaritan who gave me a lift in his pickup truck, and I worked here and there for train fare. And of course I took a boat to Hawaii."

"That must have taken you 20 years," said Sarah.

"If it had taken me 20 years," Grandpa said, "I wouldn't have been home in time to marry your grandma and to be your daddy's daddy. Nope, only took me three years. But oh, what I saw in those three years. We climbed the Statue of Liberty in New York, rode out a hurricane in Georgia, ran from an alligator in Florida, herded cattle in Texas, climbed down the Grand Canyon in Arizona, saw rock goblins in Utah, met movie stars in California, and went surfing in Hawaii. Why, in every state I

44

did something exciting. It was the best education a young man could ever get."

"Mom?" pleaded Alan.

"No!" Mom said.

"Mom?" asked Patrick.

"No!" Mom said.

"Mom?" said Nicholas, Sarah, and Davy.

"No! No! No!" said Mom.

"Yip?" Gator barked.

"Not even for you, Gator."

"It would be fun to do as a family," said Dad.

"Maybe," said Mom.

"Why, you should do it," said Grandpa. "Wish I'd taken that trip with my kids."

"Did you bring back any souvenirs?" Sarah asked.

"Didn't have much room for souvenirs," Grandpa said. "Just for memories. But I did have one special souvenir. When I left on my trip, I took an American flag: 13 stripes, 50 stars. And in every state, I visited the governor and had him sign a star. I even had the territorial governors of Hawaii and Alaska sign a star. After three years I had 50 governors' signatures on 50 stars."

"Wow," said Dad. "How come you never showed that to me?"

"When I got home after three years," said Grandpa, "I recognized just how valuable that flag was. Maybe not money value, but patriotic value. I donated it to the Smithsonian Institute in Washington DC. When you take your trip around the country, stop in. Maybe they'll show it to you."

"I vote we start planning our trip right away," said Nicholas. "Even if there is one minor flaw in Grandpa's story."

What flaw did Nicholas see? (Answer on p. 139.)

LIKE SOME DIAMONDS

IN THE SKY

A mystery for the 4th of July

"Ooh!"

"Aah!"

As the fireworks burst in the sky before them, the Arthurs applauded and cheered.

"How far away are they?" Sarah asked.

"Count the seconds between when you see the firework and when you hear its boom," Mrs. Arthur said. "Sound travels about a mile in five seconds."

They waited for the next explosion of light, and then they began to count. "Thousand one, thousand two, thou. . . ."

BOOM!

"Arf!" Gator loved the explosions.

"A little more than two seconds," Nicholas said. "We're about half a mile away."

The Paris Fork Fourth of July celebration was always very popular. Thousands of people came into town to see the parade, go to the carnival, and of course, watch the fireworks.

The fireworks were held in Centennial Park, the town's largest park, which stretched along a good portion of the east side of town. A large part of the center of the park was roped off. This was where the fireworks were lit. On both sides of the fireworks area were large expanses of grass, now covered with blankets and people.

"I wish we could be closer," Sarah said.

"I'm glad we're not," said Mrs. Arthur. "The smell of fireworks makes me sick."

The Arthurs had been helping Mr. Arthur run the Arts Festival that had been held downtown. By the time they had arrived for the fireworks, the park was almost filled with spectators. So the Arthur family sat at the end of the park, near a dark shopping center that housed a law office, a jewelry store, a game shop, a pet shop, and several more small stores.

Another burst of fireworks. "It looks like a diamond necklace!" Sarah said. "I love it!"

And then another. "A waterfall," said Mr. Arthur. "Nice."

And then a rapid burst of lights, like firecrackers

going off in the sky. It sounded funny to hear the staccato of the explosions out of sync with the lights in the sky.

And then there was silence for five, maybe ten seconds. And then...

BOOM!

"Must have been a dud," Mr. Arthur said. "It exploded, but the fireworks inside didn't light up."

Eight, maybe ten more fireworks rapidly exploded into the sky, followed by more, and more, and more. The Arthurs sat hypnotized.

While Sarah watched, Gator jumped into her lap and curled up. Sarah looked down and stroked him behind the ears.

"Hey buddy, are you enjoying the fireworks?" Sarah asked him.

Gator looked up at Sarah. That's when she noticed he had something in his mouth.

It sparkled like fireworks. She reached down and took it carefully from him. She held it up close to her face.

"It's a necklace!" she shouted. The rest of her family turned and looked at her.

"Where did you get that?" Mom asked. "Let me see it." Sarah handed it to her.

Mrs. Arthur looked at it closely. "It's hard to tell in the dark, but it looks like a real diamond necklace! Where did you find it?"

"Gator had it," Sarah said.

"Oh dear," Mrs. Arthur said. "He must have taken it from someone in the park when they weren't looking. We'll have to take it to lost and found."

Nicholas jumped up. "No, there's no time!" he said. "Dad, give me your cell phone. I need to call the police. There's been a robbery."

A confused Mr. Arthur handed Nicholas the cell phone. Nicholas dialed 911, and quickly explained to the police where and how the robbery had taken place.

Where and how did the robbery take place, and how did Nicholas know? (Answer on p. 139.)

A No-Brainer

It could be a deal that no one could refuse....

"Have I got something for you!" Travis said to Nicholas and Sarah. From behind his back he brought a huge pair of plastic glasses. Each lens was as big as his face.

Travis was the neighborhood schemer. He always had a plan for making money. And he always tried to involve others in his plans. If you were smart, you didn't get involved with any of his plans, because at best they were naïve. At worst they were frauds.

"Here," Travis said to Sarah. "Try them on."

Sarah took them and put them on her face. Gator growled at her, then barked.

"So you think I look funny," she said. "Let's see how you look with them on, Gator." She took

55

them off her head, and put one of the eyeholes over Gator's head.

Gator shook his head, but the glasses stayed on. He kept shaking, and was finally able to wiggle out of the glasses. He growled and started to chew on them.

"Stop!" Travis shouted, and he reached down and jerked the glasses away from Gator. "These are very valuable glasses! You'll ruin them!"

"What's so valuable about them?" Nicholas asked.

"What's so valuable about them?!" Travis asked in astonishment. "Why, you're looking at real live Cyclops glasses!"

"What are Cyclops glasses?" Sarah asked. "And why are they so valuable?"

"Why, Cyclops glasses were worn by that famous ancient giant, Cyclops," Travis said seriously. "They're probably the only Cyclops glasses in the whole world. They're probably worth thousands. Or millions."

"Where'd you get Cyclops glasses?" Sarah asked.

"My Uncle Randy," Travis said. "He's a famous explorer. He was exploring in some country where Cyclops used to live, and he discovered a really big house, and these glasses were in them. He brought them home and gave them to me so I could sell them and pay for my college."

"So, do you want us to buy them?" Nicholas asked.

"So close," Travis said. "So close. But I don't want *you* to buy them. I want your father to buy them for the Paris Fork Historical Museum. It's a no-brainer. It'll put the museum on the map. It'll put Paris Fork on the map. It'll make your dad famous. And I'm telling you all this why? Good question. Because I want to let you in on my good fortune. If you can get your dad to buy these very valuable glasses, I'll give you ten percent of what I make. That could be a lot of money."

Sarah smiled and clapped her hands. "I could buy a pony! Gator, we can get a pony!"

Gator just growled.

"Oh, you'll like a pony, Gator," Sarah said. "You can ride it. We will make enough money to buy a pony, won't we, Travis?"

"I'm sure you will," Travis said. "You might even make enough to buy a whole horse farm."

Gator growled louder and started advancing towards Travis. Travis took a few steps back.

Nicholas couldn't take it any longer. He broke into an uncontrollable fit of laughter. "Travis," he said, "your schemes are always unbelievable. But this one, this one is the worst one you've ever tried to pull off. And Sarah, I'm surprised you're falling for it. Even Gator isn't."

Why didn't Nicholas trust Travis's scheme? (Answer on p. 140.)

TAKING A TRIP

Gator is in trouble again!

"Yip, yarp!" Gator tugged on his leash. He wanted to run.

But Sarah didn't. "Gator, if I let you go you'll get lost again." The last time Sarah and Nicholas had taken the long walk to their father's office, Sarah had let Gator off of his leash, and they had looked for him for an hour before they found him splashing through the stream that ran through Pioneer Park.

Gator stopped, sat on his haunches, showed Sarah his saddest face, and whimpered.

Sarah couldn't resist. "Okay, Gator," she said as she stooped down to unhook his leash. "But only if you promise not to get lost again. In fact I want you to stay in sight at all times, okay?"

"If he gets lost this time," Nicholas said, "you're looking for him yourself."

"I'll watch him better this time," Sarah said. She patted Gator on the head, then stood up.

Gator jumped up and ran to the nearest bush.

"See," Sarah said, "he just had important business to attend to."

Sarah and Nicholas continued walking, slowly, looking in the shop windows, stopping from time to time to add something to their wish lists. Gator was always in sight, investigating this, sniffing that, and getting petted by an occasional passerby.

"I think it's about time I get a new bike," Nicholas said. "Like this one." He stood in front of the bike shop window, admiring the window display. "Think dad will buy me that mountain bike?"

"I think Dad will give you jobs so you can earn money to buy the bike," Sarah said. Mr. and Mrs. Arthur felt it was important that the kids earn their own spending money, and they gave them many opportunities to do so.

Nicholas began to calculate how many leaves he'd have to rake and how many weeds he'd have to pull to get that bike. "Maybe they'll get it for me for Christmas. Or my birthday."

They continued on. And then Nicholas noted, "Uh, Sarah, where's Gator?"

He was nowhere to be seen. "Ooh! That dog! When I get him. . . ."

Sarah was interrupted by a thud, a yell, and

barking from just around the corner from where they stood.

"Gator!" Sarah yelled, and she took off running.

When the kids rounded the corner, they saw a young man, getting up from the sidewalk next to the curb. He reached down, picked up his glasses, and squinted at Sarah and Nicholas. "Officers," he said. "He put his glasses back on and looked at Nicholas and Sarah. "Where did the police go?" he said. "They were right here."

"You were looking at us," Sarah said.

The young man looked around. Then he pointed at Gator, who was sitting a few feet away, looking concerned. "There he is! There's the dog that tripped me! I'm going to have him arrested and taken to the pound. Where are the police when you need them?"

"He's my dog!" Sarah said. "He's not going to the pound!"

"He's a menace!" the young man said.

"He is not!"

"Is too!"

"Is not!"

"Is too!"

"Just a minute," Nicholas interrupted. "Tell us exactly what happened. If it was Gator's fault, we'll deal with it." He gave a nasty look to Gator.

"There's an alligator here? Where!?" the young man asked, shocked. "What's wrong with this city? All of these vicious animals running around! Someone should do something about it!"

"Gator's my dog," Sarah said. "He's not a real alligator."

"Back to where we were," Nicholas said. "Tell me what happened?"

"Okay," the young man said. "I was crossing the street, I'd taken off my glasses to clean the lenses, I was thinking about what I wanted for lunch, and I was almost all the way across, when suddenly that dog," he pointed at Gator, "ran right at my feet and knocked me over. I saw him. He's a menace. Take him to the pound right away before he hurts someone else."

"I told you," Sarah said, " he's not going to the pound!"

"Is too!" the young man said.

"Is not!"

"Is too!"

"Is not!" Nicholas interrupted. "Because I can prove that Gator didn't trip you, and I know what did."

What did Nicholas know? (Answer on p. 140.)

PIECES OF PIZZA

A cooking caper of equal proportions

"Put on more pineapple," Sarah said. "I like pineapple."

"So do I," Nicholas said. "So more pineapple it is. And while we're at it, let's put on more ham."

"And lots of cheese," Sarah added. "We like cheese, don't we, Gator." She reached down and scratched Gator behind his ears.

"Lots and lots of cheese," Nicholas agreed.

Mom and Dad were both working late, their older brothers, Alan and Patrick, both had evening jobs at fast food places, and their four-year-old brother Davy was being babysat at Aunt Jo's. Aunt Jo was the mother of their favorite cousins, Joseph and Ellie. Davy stayed over there a lot.

And so Nicholas and Sarah got to make their own

dinner. And of course their first choice was pizza. They could have just ordered out, but if they made it themselves, they were sure that it would be just how they liked it.

Nicholas dumped the last of the shredded cheese on the pizza, opened the oven door, and slid the pizza into the hot oven.

"Fifteen minutes," Nicholas said.

"And then it's pizza time!" Sarah said.

"Arf!" Gator barked. He loved pizza.

While the pizza cooked, Nicholas made a salad, Sarah made juice and set the table, and Gator watched the oven door. He was going to make sure that he got his share of pizza.

DING! At the sound of the timer, Gator barked and Nicholas and Sarah jumped for the oven. Nicholas grabbed a hot pad, opened the door, and reached in. He slid out the pizza, with its perfectly browned crust and toasted cheese.

He carried it over to the table and set it on a ceramic tile so it wouldn't burn the table. Sarah brought over the pizza cutter. Gator brought himself, and his appetite.

"Cut it into thirds," Sarah said. "One for each of us."

"One for each of us?" Nicholas said. "Me and you?"

"And Gator of course," Sarah said. Gator barked in agreement.

"Of course," Nicholas said. He put the cutter up

next to the crust, ready to cut. And then he pulled it away.

"Wait a minute," he said. "What if Aunt Jo brings Davy home? He might want some pizza. We'd better cut the pizza into four slices."

"But his slice would be too big for him to hold," Sarah said. "Besides, what if Aunt Jo brings him home and he's already asleep? That sometimes happens. Or what if he's already had dinner? That happens a lot. Then he won't want any pizza. And if you cut four pieces there will be an extra piece."

"For me!" Nicholas said.

"No way!" Sarah said. "We're dividing this pizza evenly."

"Yeah," Nicholas said. "But evenly how? If I cut it in three pieces, and Davy wants one, it'll be too few. But if I cut it in four pieces, and he doesn't want one, then we'll have the fight over the fourth piece. And either way the pizza slices are probably going to be too big anyway."

Nicholas mulled over the problem for a while, but eventually he figured out how to slice the pizza so that all of the slices were the same size, and that no matter what Davy wanted, they would be able to divide the pizza evenly.

How many slices did Nicholas cut the pizza into?
(Answer on p. 140.)

KIDNAPPED

What happened to Joseph and Ellie's neighbors?

"I tell you, Nicholas, they've been kidnapped!" It was Nicholas's cousin Joseph on the phone. "Or worse!"

"I'll come right over and take a look," Nicholas said.

He hung up the phone and put on his jacket.

"Where are you going?" Sarah asked him. She was making a sandwich on the kitchen counter. Gator was standing at her feet, hoping he'd get some of the sandwich.

"Joseph and Ellie's neighbors are missing," Nicholas said. "Joseph thinks there's something wrong and wants me to come take a look." He headed for the door.

"Wait for me," Sarah said. She grabbed her

69

sandwich and slipped on her sweater. "I'm coming too."

"Arf!" Gator said, and followed after. He wanted to make sure he got part of that sandwich.

"So which neighbors are missing?" Sarah asked. She threw half of the sandwich to Gator, who gobbled it up, and she bit into the other half.

"He didn't say," Nicholas said. "He said he'd fill me in when we get there."

When they reached Joseph and Ellie's house, both of their cousins were standing in the doorway, waiting.

"Oh, Sarah," Ellie said, "something's happened to them, I'm sure of it. They're very nice. Sometimes I get their mail for them, or I pick their newspaper up off the porch for them. They'd let me in and thank me and give me cookies. I'm going to miss them."

"Now, now," Nicholas said, "we don't know that something's happen to them. For that matter, we don't even know who they are. Which neighbors are they?"

"Mr. and Mrs. Benson, next door," Joseph said. He pointed to the house on their right. "They're always out working in their yard when we go to school. But this morning I realized I hadn't seen them for a few days. I don't know how long. I looked and noticed that the fall leaves were scattered all over their yard. They wouldn't have let that happen if they were okay. They're very good about keeping their leaves raked."

"So we're sure someone's kidnapped them," Ellie said. "Or maybe they had an accident and are lying on the floor in their house, injured . . . or worse!"

"Did you call the police?" Sarah asked.

"I was going to," Ellie said, "but Joseph said you might be able to solve it faster."

"Well, we won't figure out what happened standing here," Nicholas said. He led the way to the Benson's house.

"We need to look in the garden," Ellie said. "Sometimes kidnappers bury their victims in the garden, and you can tell because there's freshly dug up dirt. Sarah, go see if there's freshly dug up dirt."

"I don't want to discover any dead bodies," Sarah said.

"Hey!" The children were stopped by the angry voice of a man next door. "Leave my paper alone!"

Gator had run to the front porch of another neighbor and begun to chew on the newspaper lying there. "Come back, Gator," Nicholas called. "You can play on the Benson's porch—there is nothing there for you to chew."

Gator ran to the front porch where Nicholas was waiting. He jumped around in the few leaves that had been blown there.

"Look for a ransom note," Joseph said.

Nicholas looked over the porch carefully. "Nothing here but leaves and Gator."

"Look on the door," Joseph said.

"Nothing," said Nicholas.

"Where else would they put a ransom note?" Joseph asked.

"The mailbox!" Ellie said. She ran to the mailbox, opened the door, and looked in. "Nothing. It's empty." She closed the door and came back to the porch.

By now Gator had pushed all of the leaves off the porch. "What if the note was in the leaves?" Ellie asked. "Or maybe Gator ate it."

"I've been watching Gator," Nicholas said. "There wasn't anything in the leaves, and he didn't eat anything. If there had been something, I would have seen him dig it up."

"Talk about digging," Ellie said, "look at Gator!" Gator was now digging furiously in the garden. "He's found something! I told you we should dig in the garden."

"No," Nicholas said. "He just likes to dig. Besides, I don't know where the Bensons are, but I'm sure they haven't been kidnapped, that they're not lying in their house, and that they are not buried in their garden. Because of a hint from Gator, I'm sure they're just fine."

Why was Nicholas so sure? (Answer on p. 140.)

VANDALISM!

What is Paris Fork coming to?

"Who'd throw that on the ground?" Sarah asked in disgust. She stopped, handed Nicholas Gator's leash, and stooped down to pick up the kid's meal sack, which was spilled over with muddy French fries and a stepped-on hamburger from the fast food place across the street.

Before she could pick up the sack though, Gator had the hamburger in his mouth. And then, it was gone. Gator licked his lips and barked.

"Gator, that was revolting!" Sarah said. "Besides, you just had lunch. You didn't need that hamburger. Nicholas, you were supposed to be holding on to him."

"I was," Nicholas said. "It's not my fault that he has a long leash. Besides, what's wrong with him eating that hamburger? He's eaten stuff much worse than that."

75

"It's just disgusting," Sarah said. She picked up the sack and fries and dropped them in a nearby garbage can.

"Now give me my dog," she told her brother.

"Gladly," Nicholas said.

"There's just too much of that these days," Sarah said.

"Too much of what?" Nicholas asked.

"Too much disrespect for property. Everywhere you look there's litter, and graffiti, and vandalism. It's because parents don't keep their kids busy enough."

"You mean kids like us?" Nicholas asked. Nicholas, Sarah, and Gator were just spending a day wandering about town, exploring. It was one of their favorite things to do in the summer. Sometimes they'd visit their dad at work, or stop in to see friends. But most of their time they just spent discovering things they'd never noticed before, like new shops and funny signs.

"Besides," Nicholas added, "you're starting to sound like Grandma. In fact, I think I heard that speech from Grandma last week."

Sarah laughed. "I am, aren't I."

The two kept walking, in silence, until Sarah spoke again. "But I am serious about it being a problem. I like Paris Fork. It's a great city."

"I like it too," Nicholas said.

Sarah continued, "And it drives me crazy when

people don't treat it right." She stopped walking. "Look at that bench, for example. Somebody scratched their name in it in big ugly letters."

"It is pretty ugly," Nicholas said.

"And look at that tree," Sarah said. "Someone broke that branch off and now it's just a sharp ugly stump."

They kept walking. And then Sarah stopped. "And look at that! That's awful! Somebody's been writing graffiti in that store window."

Nicholas looked. In the window were scrawled a bunch of what looked like nonsense words.

IMAIM
IIAWAH
ITIHAT

"Probably a gang banger," Sarah said. "Our city's starting to get overrun by gangs."

"Are you sure it's a gang banger?" Nicholas said.

"Of course," Sarah said. "Just look at it. The first line says 'I Maim.' That means he's going to hurt someone. 'Iiawah' is probably the nickname of the guy he's going to hurt. And 'Iti Hat" means the guy he's going to hurt has a little hat."

"That's silly," Nicholas said. "Why would someone want to hurt someone just because he has a little hat?"

"He doesn't want to hurt him just because he

has a little hat," Sarah insisted. "That's just how you recognize him. It's just a warning that Iiawah, the guy who wears a little hat, needs to watch out."

"What do you think Gator?" Nicholas asked. "Have you seen any gangsters around recently?"

Gator barked, then pawed at the shop door.

"You have the right idea, Gator," Nicholas said. "We need to point something out to my sister." He pointed to the sign above the window. "Let's go in so I can show Sarah something that will solve this mystery."

What did Nicholas show Sarah inside the store? (Answer on p. 141.)

THE ELECTRIC GHOST

Is Sarah's computer really haunted?

"Hiding, hiding, in your house,
Who's that clicking on the mouse?
No one knows what she sees,
Who's that tapping on the keys?"

"Make that up yourself, Nicholas?" said Sarah without turning away from her typing.

"I've been standing here for five minutes waiting for you to notice me," said Nicholas. "I've had plenty of time to compose my brilliant poem."

"Oh, I knew it was you. Could the clue have been hearing Mom shout, 'Nicholas, go find Sarah and tell her it's time for dinner?' I was just trying to ignore you. This story's due tomorrow, and Gator's doing his best to make sure I don't get it written." Gator looked up and barked when he heard his name. But now . . . it's . . . DONE!" and she clicked on "Print."

"I would have had it done lots earlier," Sarah said, "but Patrick and Alan tied up the computer all day. Alan was the worst. He kept kicking me out." Alan and Patrick were Sarah and Nicholas's older brothers.

"And then the computer kept crashing on me," said Sarah, "like it was haunted or something."

Sarah and Gator followed Nicholas in to dinner. When they were through, Nicholas said, "Who wants to play Clue?"

"I'll play," said Sarah. "But I'd better get my story into my backpack first." She was gone from the kitchen for just a minute when the family heard a scream.

Everyone raced to the computer room where Sarah stood, frozen and white. "L-l-l-look!" She pointed at the computer screen. On it were big white words on a black background. The words read:

HELLO SARAH—I AM THE ELECTRIC GHOST

The words faded, and new words appeared:

I KNOW WHERE YOU LIVE. I SEE WHAT YOU DO.

And then new words appeared:

I AM COMING TO GET YOU! BWAH-HAH-HAH-HAH-HAH!

"H-h-h-help," whimpered Sarah. "My computer *is* haunted."

The screen went black, and then the message began again.

"I knew there was something spooky about you," said Alan.

"Cool!" Patrick said.

"That is awfully weird," Mom said.

"Probably just a computer virus," said Dad. "I'll take it into the shop tomorrow."

"Arooo!" Gator said. He jumped on the chair and started pawing the keyboard . . .

. . . and the message disappeared.

"You killed it!" said Nicholas. "Gator, you killed the ghost!" And then, very solemnly, he said, "but I bet he'll be back before long."

"You think so?" said Sarah.

"I know so," said Nicholas. He looked around the room. "Because I know where he came from."

What did Nicholas know? (Answer on p. 141.)

FAST! EEE!

THE SNOWMAN!

Nicholas and Sarah's snow family doesn't even compare...

"There's never a carrot around when you need one," said Sarah. "I need a nose."

"Gator, fetch a stick!" Nicholas said. Gator did as he was told, and soon the snowman had a stick nose.

"Perfect!" said Nicholas. "The family's done."

Nicholas and Sarah had taken advantage of the deep snowfall of the night before. They'd built an entire snow family. Mom, Dad, brother, sister, baby, a dog that looked like Gator, even a bird sitting on a tree branch.

Mrs. Arthur poked her head out of the house. "Nicholas, phone's for you." She handed Nicholas the cordless phone.

"Frosty here."

"Come see the cool snowman I made!" said Joseph, on the other end. "He's out of sight, and you'll never guess where I built it!"

"We'll be right there. Then you have to come see our snow family." Nicholas overheard Aunt Jo in the background. "Joseph, I'll be right back. I've got to run some errands."

"All right, Mom," said Joseph. "Sounds good, Nicholas, I'll see you in a couple of minutes."

Nicholas, Sarah, and Gator headed off for Joseph's house. All along the way they saw other sculptures. Lots of normal snowmen, but also a few creative works. A snowman standing on his head, a snow baby in a swing, a snow dog lying on a porch.

Gator barked at the snow dog. The snow dog barked back. The kids jumped, then laughed. They could have sworn that white dog was made of snow.

They turned down Joseph's street, a major road divided down the middle with a high, snow-covered hedge.

Half a block down the street, Nicholas and Sarah stopped and stared. The barking snow dog had surprised them, but this was impossible.

There, on the other side of the hedge, was a snowman. And he was alive! He raced along, past the kids, and away.

"Did you see that?" asked Nicholas.

"A living snowman?" said Sarah. "Corn cob pipe? Button nose? Two eyes made out of coal? And an old silk hat?"

"It's Frosty!" they said together.

"We have to tell Joseph!" said Sarah.

"He won't believe us," said Nicholas.

"I don't believe it," Sarah said.

The kids ran the block down to Joseph's house. They plowed through the deep snow on the lawn while Gator took the easy route, along the tire tracks in the driveway. Nicholas knocked on the door. Joseph opened it.

"THE SNOWMAN!" Nicholas and Sarah blurted out.

Joseph interrupted them. "Cool, isn't he." He stepped out into the yard. "Bet you wonder how I . . . he's gone?"

"Who's gone?" said Sarah.

"My snowman," said Joseph. He was silent for a moment, then he smiled, and then laughed. "Oh no! Don't tell me!"

"Your snowman," said Sarah. "Was he wearing a silk hat?"

"Yes," said Joseph.

"We saw him racing down your street," said Sarah. "You built a live snowman! How'd you do it?"

"I know how," said Nicholas.

What did Nicholas know? (Answer on p. 141.)

EGG-ZACTLY

A breakfast blunder.

"I wish Mom were home," Nicholas said as he finished unloading the dishwasher.

"Why?" Sarah asked. "So she could do your dishes?"

"No, so she could make breakfast."

"My breakfast is going to be perfectly good," Sarah said. She reached for a pot out of the dishwasher.

"What are we having?" Nicholas asked.

"Arf arp?" Gator barked. He wanted to know what leftovers he was going to be eating.

Sarah began to fill the pot with water. "Hard-boiled eggs and toast," she said.

"Yip!" Gator loved eggs boiled, fried, scrambled, or raw. He leaped at Sarah's legs.

"Gator, out of my way," Sarah said. "If I trip you're going to be one wet dog."

She took the pot over to the counter, carefully placed six eggs in it, and set the pot on the stove.

"If Mom were here we'd be having waffles," Nicholas said. "Or omelets."

"Well, Mom's not here," Sarah said. "So unless you want to make breakfast yourself, quit complaining."

Although Sarah and Nicholas had the summer off, Mr. and Mrs. Arthur still had jobs, and needed to be to work. Their older brothers had worked late last night, and besides, they were teenagers, so they probably wouldn't be up until early afternoon.

So Nicholas, Sarah, and Gator were having breakfast alone. They could have had breakfast with their parents, but then they would have had to get up early, and somehow that was something they hadn't wanted to do on this lazy summer day.

"Hey everybody. Is anybody awake?" A small voice came from the stairs.

"Davy!" Nicholas and Sarah said at the same time. "Good morning!" They ran to give their brother a hug. "How are you doing?" Sarah asked. Gator licked Davy's face.

"Good," Davy said. "Is it breakfast time yet?"

"Not yet," Sarah said. "The eggs are cooking."

"Yum! I like eggs!" Davy said.

"Yip!" Gator said.

Sarah turned to Nicholas. "See! Davy and Gator like my cooking."

"Davy and Gator like everyone's cooking," Nicholas said.

"Turn on cartoons?" Davy said.

"Cartoons!" Nicholas and Sarah said together. They rushed to the living room, Sarah turned on the TV, and they plopped onto the couch. Gator jumped into Sarah's lap and watched along, barking whenever another dog came onto the screen.

The kids watched for some time, until Davy said, "Is my egg ready?"

Gator heard the word "egg," jumped off Sarah's lap, and ran into the kitchen.

"Wait until a commercial and I'll check," Sarah said.

"But I'm hungry now!" Davy said.

"Oh, all right," Sarah said. "I'll get the eggs if Nicholas helps me make the toast."

"I thought you were making breakfast." Nicholas said.

"Come on, Nicholas, please? I don't want to miss any of this cartoon. Please, second favorite brother ever?"

"Oh, all right," Nicholas said. Sarah smiled and headed for the kitchen, keeping her eye on the television the whole time.

Nicholas and Davy followed after her.

It was a little tricky, but Sarah could watch the TV from the stove. She had to twist her head and lean way back, but even as she reached into the pot and pulled out an egg, she didn't miss a second of the show.

"I'll have this peeled for you in just a second, Davy," she said.

"Uh, Sarah," Nicholas said, "I don't think you want try to peel that egg, unless you want to have to clean up a big mess."

"Rarf!" said Gator, who sat at Sarah's feet, looking up. He thought a big mess of egg sounded delicious.

Why did Nicholas think Sarah was about to make a mess? (Answer on p. 142.)

AN ICE SURPRISE

The magic fairies
have come out to play!

The break in the cold weather was wonderful.
The kids played outside in shorts and T-shirts. They
rolled in the grass and chased Gator through the
bushes. They couldn't have done this just two days
ago when the ground was covered with snow.

But it couldn't last forever. One night, winter
returned.

The next morning, after rolling out of bed and
eating a hot breakfast, Nicholas, Sarah, and Davy put
on their coats and boots and ran out to the backyard
to play in the snow. Gator tromped after them. He
already had his coat on.

And then they stopped and stared in awe.

"Lookie!" said Davy.

"Wow!" said Sarah.

There before them was an ice palace. Flows of ice cascaded down the bushes in their yard.

"It's magic!" said Sarah.

"It's a magic fairy palace! There are magic fairies living in our yard!" Davy said. "Let's go find them!" And he headed for the palace.

Sarah and Gator followed him. They found a gap in the ice and crawled in under the bush. "Come on, Nicholas," Sarah said. "There's room for all of us."

Nicholas climbed in with them. They sat and stared at the sunlight streaming through the ice. It was like living in diamonds.

"Let's go show Mommy," said Davy. "Maybe she can help us find the magic fairies."

They ran back into the house and dragged Mrs. Arthur out. "My goodness! It's beautiful!" she said.

"Climb in with us," Sarah said.

"I don't think I'll fit," said Mrs. Arthur.

"Sure you will," Sarah said, and she led her into the ice palace. Soon the palace was crowded with three kids, a mother, and a dog.

"Wow!" Mrs. Arthur said as she stared at the light shining through the ice.

"Let's show Dad," said Davy.

They all crawled out of the palace and went back into the house to look for their father.

He wasn't there.

"The magic fairies kidnapped him," said Nicholas.

"Oh no! We have to save Daddy!" Davy said. "Find Daddy, Gator!"

Gator barked, and then ran off around the house. "Gator knows where Dad is," Sarah said. And she took off after him. Everyone followed.

There was their dad, in the garage. The magic fairies hadn't kidnapped him after all.

Dad was hanging tools back up on the wall. He was just hanging up a sprinkler head when the kids walked in.

"You've got to see this, Dad!" Sarah said.

"Yeah, Dad!" Davy said. "Magic fairies made an ice castle in our yard! Come see! Come see!" And he grabbed Dad's hand and started to pull.

But before Davy could go far, he tripped over Gator, who was wrestling with a garden hose lying on the garage floor.

"Gator, you tripped me! Davy said. He picked himself up, grabbed Dad's hand again, and continued on.

"See, Dad!" Davy said. "It's pretty!"
"Very pretty," Dad said.

"I think it was made by magic fairies. Did you see the magic fairies, Dad? Where are they?"

"Could be magic fairies," Dad said. "Or it could just be an accident of nature. Things like this do happen, I've heard."

"Or it could have been the neighbors," Mom said.

"Maybe they brought it over."

"No," said Davy. "It was magic fairies."

"It's pretty obvious that. . . . " Nicholas began. And then he changed his mind. "I'm sure it was magic fairies," he said, even though he knew where the ice palace had really come from.

How did the ice palace really get there? And how did Nicholas know? (Answer on p. 142.)

EARTHQUAKE!

Here comes the big one...

"Looks like the big one's coming soon," Mr. Arthur said from over his newspaper.

"The big what?" Sarah asked. She was lying on the floor doing her homework.

"Earthquake," said her dad.

Sarah jumped up. "Earthquake! Where? When? Where do we go? What do we do?"

Gator jumped up too, and started barking.

"Settle down," Mr. Arthur said.

"Exactly how soon is soon?" Nicholas asked, looking over the book he was reading.

"Sometime in the next five hundred years," Dad said.

"Dad! You scared me!" Sarah said. "I thought you meant the earthquake could come tomorrow. Or today."

"But it could come today," Nicholas said, "couldn't it, Dad."

"That's what they mean," Dad said. "The earthquake could come in 500 years. Or it could come tonight."

"AHHHHH! I'm not listening!" Sarah said.

"Oh, don't worry," Dad said. "We have a sturdy house. It won't fall in on us."

"Unless it's a really big earthquake," Nicholas said.

"Nicholas! Stop it!" Sarah said.

"I think it's time for you both to stop," Dad said, "and head off to bed. It's late."

"Later than you think," Nicholas said. "Are you ready for the big one?"

"NICHOLAS!" Sarah yelled.

Sarah brushed her teeth and combed her hair. Then she filled a glass of water a little too full—she sometimes got thirsty in the night—and carried it carefully to her room. Gator followed her in.

Sarah set the water gently on her nightstand, put on her pajamas, laid her clothes on her chair, arranged her stuffed tiger next to her pillow, turned off her light, and crawled under her covers.

Gator jumped on the bed and curled up at her feet.

And soon they were both asleep.

And then, in the middle of the night, Sarah began to dream that she was on a roller coaster, up and down, back and forth. And Gator was on the roller coaster with her, barking furiously. When did they start letting dogs ride roller coasters? Sarah was afraid he'd fall out.

Then the roller coaster began to fade away, but the shaking and the barking did not. And then Sarah awoke with a start and realized what was happening.

"EARTHQUAKE!" she screamed.

And then suddenly the shaking stopped, and a second later the light came on. There at the door stood Nicholas. "Did you feel it?" he asked. "Did you feel the earthquake?"

Gator barked at Nicholas.

"Yeah, boy. You felt it didn't you," Nicholas said. "It was cool, wasn't it. I told you the big one would come soon, Sarah," he said.

She tried to calm herself. She was still shaking a bit. She steadied her hand and then reached for her glass of water. She raised it to her mouth, careful not to spill, sipped some of the water off the top, then took a big drink.

And then she looked around her room. Her tiger was on the floor. Her chair and her clothes were tipped over. Books had fallen from her bookshelf.

"Some mess, huh?" Nicholas said. "You should see my room. It's even messier."

Sarah took another drink of water. And then she set her glass back down on the nightstand.

"Nicholas," she said, "your room's always messier than mine. But don't blame an earthquake, because there wasn't one."

How did Sarah know? (Answer on p. 142.)

THE THIEF IN THE SHADOW

Can the police find the prize painting?

"Who's in the mood for pizza?" Mr. Arthur asked.

"I am!" said Nicholas.

"You need to ask?" said Sarah.

"Arf!" said Gator.

"Then everyone in the car."

It was Dad's turn to cook. Mrs. Arthur was out of town. Her job as a freelance computer programmer often took her away.

Nicholas dove for the front seat.

"I get the front on the way back," Sarah said.

"Arf," said Gator.

"No dogs allowed in the front," Dad said.

Dad weaved his way through the streets of Paris

Fork then pulled to a stop in front of the Paris Fork Art Museum.

"So, they're serving pizza at the museum now?" said Nicholas.

"No," said Dad. "I just need to stop for a minute here. One of the paintings was stolen. The police are on it, but I just want to check it out."

"Which painting?" Sarah asked.

"'Whitman's Dog.' It was the museum's prize painting—a portrait of a famous poet with his dog, who looked just like Gator."

Mr. Arthur was the manager of the Paris Fork Arts Council. He wasn't in charge of the museum, but he was in charge of the woman who was in charge of the museum.

Before Dad could get out of the car, Nicholas and Sarah had thrown open their doors and jumped out, along with Gator.

"You don't have to come," said Dad.

"Sure we do," said Nicholas. "A crime's been committed. We need to see it."

"Maybe we can solve it," said Sarah.

"Arf," said Gator.

"All right," said Dad. "Come along."

The museum was in the shape of a large U. In the center was a spacious courtyard, with paths, benches, and statues. In the center of the courtyard was a large statue of a woman holding a flag.

Sarah, Nicholas and Gator headed straight for the bench in front of statue. As they sat, the late afternoon sun behind them made the woman's face glow. The shadow behind her reached all the way to the museum wall.

"Big Lady Drying Her Laundry," said Nicholas

"Hitchhiker Flagging down a Truck," said Sarah.

It was their favorite game at the museum, coming up with new names for the statue. The real name, the name on the plaque at the base of the statue of the woman holding a flag was, "Woman Holding a Flag." Nicholas and Sarah thought the artist could have been more original.

"Arf!"

"Coming, Gator," said Nicholas, and he and Sarah jumped up and followed Gator, who was following Mr. Arthur into the museum.

They caught up with their dad in the big hall, where the pride of the museum's exhibit was, or used to be anyway. There was a big blank space right in front of them. Next to the blank space were two police officers, Mrs. Williams the museum curator, and Jack, the morning museum guard. The police officers were dusting, measuring, and taking notes.

Mr. Arthur ducked under the yellow crime scene tape that surrounded the area. Sarah and Nicholas ducked in after him. Gator didn't have to duck.

Jack rushed up to Mr. Arthur. "He was behind

the Woman Holding a Flag, hiding in her shadow, when I came in this morning. As I passed the statue he jumped up and ran out of the courtyard. He was carrying a long tube."

"Jack called me right away when he saw the painting was missing," said Mrs. Williams. "And I called the police."

"Was the museum door unlocked when you got here?" asked Nicholas.

"No," said Jack. "He must have stolen a key."

"We'll get the locks all changed right away," said Mrs. Williams.

Gator was very interested in what the police were doing. Or what one of the policeman's flashlights was doing. As the officer ran the light over the scene, looking closely for clues, Gator chased it. The officer tried to shoo Gator away, but Gator just thought that was part of the game.

"How come the police are just now looking for clues," Sarah asked, "if the painting was stolen this morning?"

"Jack gave a good description of the thief," said Mrs. Williams. "The police have been looking all over town for him. They didn't find him though."

"Of course not," said Nicholas. "They were looking in the wrong place."

The police officers immediately stopped what they were doing and turned to Nicholas.

"And where should we be looking?" the officer with a flashlight asked.

Where should they look? And how did Nicholas know? (Answer on p. 143.)

Treed

The cat is stuck and the ladder is too heavy....

"Gator! Stop it!" Ellie shouted.

Gator was chasing Porky, Ellie's cat. Gator loved to chase things. "Stop him, Sarah! Stop him!" Ellie pleaded.

Sarah ran after Gator. "Gator, heel! Heel, boy!"

"He's never done that. He doesn't even know what 'heel' means!" Nicholas said.

"There's always a first time," Sarah said. "Heel, Gator, heel!"

This wasn't going to be the first time. Gator kept chasing Porky.

Across the lawn went Porky.

Across the lawn went Gator.

Through the bushes went Porky.

Through the bushes went Gator.

Up a tree went Porky.

Gator stopped. He was a talented dog, but one thing he couldn't do was climb trees. He sat at the base of the tree and barked.

The lowest branch on the tree was quite a ways up. Porky crawled onto it and sat, shivering.

"Naughty dog, Gator!" Sarah said when she caught up to him. She grabbed him by the collar and dragged him away from the tree. "Leave that poor kitty alone."

Ellie went to the base of the tree, reached up to Porky, and said, "Come on kitty, it's okay. Come down, Porky. You can jump. I'll catch you."

Porky didn't jump. She just pressed against the tree and shivered.

"Joseph, come get her down," Ellie asked her brother.

"And how am I supposed to do that? I can't climb that tree."

"Then get a ladder."

"We don't have any ladders," Joseph said.

"We do," Sarah said. "Nicholas, run home and get our ladder."

"It's a huge ladder, Sarah," Nicholas said. "Dad uses it to climb on top of the house."

"Good," Sarah said. "Then it's big enough to get Porky out of the tree."

"It's also too heavy for me to carry," Nicholas said.

"Then take Joseph to help you."

"That ladder is really, really heavy," Nicholas said. "Let's see if we can find an easier way to get Porky down."

"Let's throw something at her," Joseph said. "We can scare her down."

"Joseph!" Ellie was appalled at his suggestion. "No. I know. Joseph, stand next to the tree."

"And then Porky can climb down on me," Joseph said as he positioned himself under the tree.

"No," said Sarah. "Now, Nicholas, climb on Joseph's shoulders. Then you'll be tall enough to reach Porky."

"Ouch," said Joseph. "He's heavy!"

"Hey!" Nicholas said. "I weigh the same as you. You're just taller than me." Joseph was taller, and skinnier. And his long arms and legs made him look even taller than he really was.

"Oh, all right," Joseph said. "Climb on."

Nicholas stepped into Joseph's clasped hands, and Joseph boosted him up onto his shoulders. They wobbled a bit and looked like they might fall, but Nicholas was able to grab the tree and steady himself.

"Now get Porky," Ellie said.

Nicholas reached up. As far as he could. He stretched his arms as high as he could. But it wasn't enough. He was just a few inches from reaching Porky.

He hopped down.

"Let's try it again," Joseph said. "Only this time take a broom with you. You can swat Porky out of the tree."

"JOSEPH!" Ellie wasn't happy with his suggestion.

"I don't think we have to go that far," Nicholas said. "Let's try it again. We won't need to use something to swat Porky, but we will have to do something just a little different."

They did do something just a little different, and it worked. Porky was soon safe in Ellie's arms.

What did they do this time? (Answer on p. 143.)

SUNDAY FUNNIES

(and waffle sundaes)

Sunday morning at the Arthur house was the family's favorite morning. Mostly because of Sunday breakfast.

It was a family tradition. On the menu—waffle sundaes, of course. Hot, crisp waffles, piled high with ice cream, topped with fruit sauces, marshmallow topping, and nuts.

This Sunday, the first day of the month, Nicholas had finished off two—one blueberry almond waffle sundae, one strawberry peanut waffle sundae.

Sarah had chosen chocolate and chocolate.

"Have another?" Mrs. Arthur asked Nicholas. She held out a platter stacked high with waffles.

"My tongue says yes," said Nicholas. "My stomach says no. Thanks, Mom. That was delicious."

"How about you, Gator?" asked Mrs. Arthur.

"Rowff!" Gator said approvingly.

Mrs. Arthur put four waffles on Gator's plate then sprayed on some whipped cream. Gator dove in.

Nicholas and Sarah cleaned up their dishes then lay on the living room floor with the paper.

Nicholas had the comics.

Sarah had the entertainment section.

Gator came in and started chewing on the sports section.

"If you're still hungry, Gator, there are more waffles." Sarah said.

Nicholas found a couple of comics that were drop-dead hilarious, and he shared them with Sarah. The rest he read in silence.

Finally, he finished reading the comics, then turned on his side and looked at Sarah. "Anything at the movies this week?" He asked.

"Nothing I want to see," said Sarah. "Just movies about kissing and blowing things up."

"Kissing and blowing things up at the same time? That could be dangerous. Anything else?"

"No," said Sarah. "No, wait a minute. Here's something. It's not this week, but it looks fun. A free concert! First 1000 callers to 555-3665 get to go to the Rock City Megaconcert!" Sarah named the participating bands.

"Sounds fun!" said Nicholas. "When is it?"

"It says it's the fifth Saturday in April! That's this

month! Wanna go?"

"Arf!" Gator barked.

"Sorry, Gator," Sarah said. "I don't think dogs are allowed."

"I don't think anyone else will be there either," Nicholas said.

Why not? (Answer on p. 143.)

WHERE'S DAVY?

Can Nicholas, Sarah, and Mrs. Arthur find him?

"Have you seen Davy?" Mrs. Arthur asked Sarah and Nicholas, who were in the living room watching TV.

"He was right here, Mom," Sarah said.

"I think he got up to get a drink," Nicholas said.

"Well, he never came into the kitchen," Mrs. Arthur said. "Will you two help me find him?"

"Sure," the two kids said.

"I'll look in his room," said Nicholas.

"I'll check outside," Sarah offered.

"I'll look through the rest of the house," said Mrs. Arthur.

Five minutes later they were back in the kitchen without Davy. "I'm getting a little worried," said Mrs. Arthur. "It's not like him to run off like this."

"It's not?" asked Nicholas. "What about the time we found him at the Duncan's looking at their goldfish?"

"Or the time he climbed up that tree we thought he couldn't climb because there was a cat up there?" Sarah said.

"Okay," Mrs. Arthur said. "So it is like him. But we need to find him. I'll call around the neighborhood. You two look through the house again more carefully. Look in things, under things, and any place a little boy might fit.

"I have an idea," Sarah said to Nicholas after their mom had left to phone. She went to the front door, opened it, and stepped out into the yard. "Gator! Oh Gator!" She paused for a moment, and then around the corner of the house came a flash of brown. Gator leaped up the porch steps and into Sarah's arms. She scratched him behind the ears and said "Good dog!"

She put Gator down, and then said, "Where's Davy? Go find Davy, boy."

Gator started sniffing around the porch. Then he moved out into the yard. He checked out the rosebushes and the trees. And then he headed toward the corner of the house. Nicholas and Sarah followed.

Around the house Gator went and into the back yard. He sniffed around the back porch, under the swing set, along the fence, and then headed towards the bushes in the back corner of the yard. He crawled into them, and then started barking.

"Do you think. . . ." Sarah said to Nicholas.

"Let's look," Nicholas said. They crawled into the bushes after Gator.

There, curled up in the back, was Davy. "You found him, Gator! Good dog! Come on, Davy," Sarah said. "Mom's really worried about you."

In the kitchen, Mom hugged her youngest child and then got a stern look on her face. "You scared us, Davy. You need to tell us where you're going. What were you doing back there anyway?"

"I was playing with my friend," Davy said.

"Your friend?" Mom asked. "Which one?"

"My best friend," Davy said.

"Yes, but what's his name?"

"You know."

"I don't know."

"Yes you do."

"Let me try, Mom," Nicholas said. "Davy, where does he live?"

"By us," Davy said.

"There aren't any little boys who live by us," Nicholas said. "How old is he? What does he look like?"

"I don't know how old he is," Davy said. "And he looks like himself."

"I think his friend is invisible," Sarah said. "Davy

has an imaginary friend."

"He is not invisible!" Davy said. "You see him all the time. He played with me. We played hide and seek. We hid really good. I told him to be really quiet and he was really quiet."

Nicholas thought for a moment, and then he smiled. "Davy, I think I know who your friend is.

When Nicholas told him, Davy said, "Yeah! That's him! He's my best friend."

Who was Davy's friend? (Answer on p. 143.)

RIDE 'EM GRANDPA!
A history of horsemanship

"The Pony Express was the fastest mail delivery service between the east to west from April 1830 to October 1861. The riders changed horses at stations every 10 to 12 miles." Nicholas read from a sign at the Paris Fork Living History Farm. "Wow, that would take a lot of horses."

"Come catch up, Nicholas," Sarah called. She, Grandpa Arthur, Davy, and Gator had already walked to the next pony corral.

"We have a long history of horsemen in our family," Grandpa Arthur was saying as he leaned on the fence. He patted a pony on the nose then reached in his pocket for a handful of pellets that he'd bought from a vending machine at the farm. He reached the pellets out to the pony, who started licking them up. And then. . . .

"Yeow!" Grandpa jerked his arm back. His hand was missing! "That pony ate my hand! I hate when that happens."

"Grandpa," Sarah said with mild disgust mixed with amusement.

Grandpa poked his hand up through the sleeve where he'd hidden it. "Can't get one past you, can I, Sarah-bear." Grandpa was always pulling tricks and exaggerating. He loved teasing his grandkids.

"But you had better watch that dog of yours," Grandpa said, "or that pony will indeed eat him."

Sarah pulled on Gator's leash. Pets were allowed on the farm, but only on leashes. And they were supposed to stay away from the farm animals. Gator barked at the pony, but the pony ignored him.

"So, who's up for a pony ride?" Grandpa said. "We've got to continue our family horsey tradition. Sarah? Davy? I think Nicholas is a little too big for the pony ride." Grandpa led the way to the pony ride area. Six ponies were fastened to bars that rotated around a pole. On the ponies were six kids. It wasn't very exciting, but it was the most horse riding that most kids had ever done.

Grandpa led the kids to the line.

"Can Gator ride with me?" Davy asked.

"I'm afraid Gator's not allow on the ponies," Grandpa said. "Although I don't know why. Back when I was a kid my dogs used to always ride with me. Did I ever tell you about my riding days? I spent a summer herding cattle. Okay, so it wasn't as exciting as it sounded. I worked on a small farm with a few cows. But every morning I'd hop on my pony and chase the cows out to the pasture, and every evening I'd hop on my pony and chase the cows back in. Horse riding came naturally to me."

The next set of riders climbed onto their ponies and the line moved ahead. "I get the white one," Sarah said.

"I want the brown one," Davy said.

"There are three brown ones," Nicholas said.

"I want that littlest brown one," Davy said. "He's just my size. Which one are you going to ride, Nicholas?"

"I'll just stay here and hold Gator."

"Nicholas is a big boy now," Grandpa said. "He's ready for the big horses. Why, I'll bet he'd be good on them. Maybe even win some prizes. It's in his blood. My great-grandfather trained horses for the British royal family. When my grandfather immigrated to the America, his first job was with the Pony Express. He rode with the Pony Express for twenty years. He had to quit, though, when cars put the Pony Express out of business."

"I want a pony," Sarah said.

Grandpa continued. "And then my father raced horses for a wealthy farmer. The horsemanship tradition skipped your father, though. He'd draw horses, he'd write about horses, but we could never get him on one."

The line had been moving forward, and it was Sarah and Davy's turn to ride. Sarah raced to the white horse, and Davy climbed on a small gray horse. He'd changed his mind. Nicholas held Gator, who tugged on his leash, not understanding why he couldn't ride too."

All the kids were strapped on, the pony ride operator checked to make sure no one was going to fall off, and away they went, around and around the pole.

Nicholas and Grandpa leaned against the fence, watching the riders. "Grandpa," Nicholas said, "How much horsemanship do we really have in our family?"

"Now son, I just told you. And a lot of the women were good with horses too."

Nicholas smiled at Grandpa. "I'm sure they were, Grandpa. But I have my doubts about at least one of my horsemen ancestors. I think you're making things up again."

Grandpa smiled at Nicholas. "I figured you'd catch me on that."

Which horse story did Nicholas know was made up? And why? (Answer on p. 143.)

NOT SO CLEAN GETAWAY

Is the stranger a gardener or a thief?

"So, what am I getting for my birthday?" Sarah asked her brother as they walked down University Avenue, followed by Gator, who kept stopping to sniff things.

"How should I know?" Nicholas said.

"You see things. You hear things. You figure things out," Sarah said. "So tell me, am I getting a pony?"

"Where would we keep a pony?" Nicholas said. He stepped aside to let an old lady pass, and then swerved around a man leaning against a lamppost.

"You didn't say I'm *not* getting a pony," Sarah said. "That means *I am* getting a pony!" She started jumping up and down and clapping her hands.

"I did *not* say you were getting a pony!"

"But I am, aren't I," Sarah insisted.

"I don't know. . . ." but Nicholas's sentence was interrupted by a loud alarm. Nicholas and Sarah turned. Gator barked.

"What is it?" Sarah asked.

"I think . . . I think," Nicholas paused then he continued, "I think the bank's just been robbed!"

Just then a man carrying a gym bag ran out of the bank, followed closely by another man. From the uniform the second man wore, it looked like he was the bank guard. He was shouting, "Stop him! Stop him!"

The robber turned right and headed away from Nicholas and Sarah.

Sarah and Nicholas were stunned.

But not as stunned as they would be in just a moment, for as the robber was escaping, the man who had been leaning against the lamppost also took off, straight for Sarah and Nicholas. Before they had a chance to move, he bowled them over, knocking them to the ground.

Gator was normally a pleasant, happy dog. But not now. He barked and took off after the man. Nicholas and Sarah were soon on their feet and running after them.

Gator leaped and came down right between the man's legs. The man tripped and went flying into some bushes by the side of the road.

A second later Nicholas and Sarah were there, next to Gator. Sarah reached down and picked up a new work glove that had fallen out of the man's pocket.

"Is he unconscious?" Sarah asked.

"I think he is," Nicholas said.

They looked at the man. Blue shirt, brown pants, both clean and pressed. On his feet were work boots. Gator licked the soles of one of the boots. "Gator, stop that!" Sarah shouted. "You don't know where those shoes have been."

"They look clean," Nicholas said. "Gator's eaten worse than that."

Just then they heard a groan, and the man began to stir.

"What should we do?" Sarah asked. "When he wakes up he might be mad at us for tripping him."

"We didn't tripped him," Nicholas said. "Gator did."

"Yeah, but Gator's our dog!"

"He's more your dog than mine," Nicholas said. "Besides, we have to stay here and watch him. He was probably involved in the bank robbery. You saw how he ran."

"You say he was involved in the bank robbery?" a voice behind them said. The kids turned. There stood a police officer.

"Why aren't you chasing the robber?" Sarah asked. "He went the other way."

"Oh, we already caught him," the officer said. "I saw the commotion up here and came to check it out. So, do you know anything about this guy? "

"We don't," Nicholas said. "But he looks awfully suspicious. He started running right after the robbery."

The man sat up and rubbed his head. "I was not involved in the robbery."

"Then why were you standing by the bank?" Nicholas asked.

"I've been doing gardening all day," the man said. "You don't think the city's gardens look the way they do all by themselves, do you? I was just taking a break."

"So why did you run?" Nicholas asked.

"Because I have a police record," he said. "And if the police found me there, they'd think I was involved."

"I think they'll find that you were involved anyway," Nicholas said. "Otherwise you wouldn't be lying to us."

What was the lie, and how did Nicholas know? (Answer on p. 144.)

Answers

Dragon (pp. 5–9)

When the culprit was being taken away, Bob reminded him to take his jacket. Yet Bob said he had never seen the young man before, and the young man had put his jacket on the bench before Bob had arrived. How did Bob know it was his jacket? Because he knew the young man. They were a team. Bob took the young dragon and had given it to his collaborator, who was then supposed to carry it out of the zoo, sell it, and split the money with Bob. Instead, Nicholas, Sarah, and Gator got treated to lunch at the zoo snack bar as a reward for Nicholas solving the crime.

What a Bite! (pp. 11–13)

If the man had just been bitten yesterday, the wound wouldn't have scarred up already. When the man saw that the game was up, he dropped Gator and ran. Sarah started to say "Sic him, Gator!" But her dad stopped her just in time.

WEST SIDE STORY (pp. 15–17)

When the kids reached University Avenue, they were facing east. Step three said, "Go south two blocks." They turned left. But if they had been facing east, south would have been to their right. After figuring out their mistake, they found the New Vibes building easily.

A BARGAIN (pp. 19–22)

Mark Twain and Lewis Carroll didn't go by those names until they were adults. When they were children, their names were Samuel Clemens and Charles Lutwidge Dodgson. And there was another problem. There was no way that the great-grandfather would have known the young Ben Franklin, who was born in 1706, and young Mark Twain, who was born in 1835.

PURPLE POND PARK (pp. 25–28)

Nicholas knew that if the boy hadn't taken the tube, when Davy said "best owl" the boy would have thought he'd said, "best towel," which is more likely to be at Purple Pond Park than an owl.

GATOR AID (pp. 31–34)

The boy had said that Sarah had broken her funny bone. But the funny bone isn't bone, it's a place on your arm where a nerve crosses over the bone. If you hit it hard, it will make your arm tingle, but you can't break it. The boy had been trying to trick the kids into leaving their pizza behind, so he could take it. But Nicholas and Gator were too smart, and too hungry, to be tricked.

HAPPY BIRTHDAY TO...
WHAT WAS THAT!? (pp. 37–40)

They'd seen that the gunfire was just bubble wrap, which Uncle James had stepped on on his way to get a midnight cake snack.

STARRY STATES (pp. 43–46)

Grandpa couldn't have had the territorial governors sign a star, because only states are represented by a star on the flag. Hawaii and Alaska didn't become states until 1958. When Grandpa took his trip, there were only 48 states, and therefore only 48 stars on the flag.

LIKE SOME DIAMONDS IN THE SKY (pp. 49–52)

Nicholas realized that the BOOM without the burst of light hadn't been a firework, but a break-in. Thieves had decided to take advantage of the fireworks explosions to hide their own explosion into the jewelry store wall. Curious Gator, though, had borrowed part of the thieves loot. Thanks to Gator's quick thinking, and Nicholas's quick thinking, the police showed up at the jewelry story just as the thieves brought out their last load.

A NO-BRAINER (pp. 55–57)

This scheme was so blatantly bad, so obviously a fraud, that Nicholas was surprised Travis even tried it. There were several reasons they couldn't have been Cyclops glasses: 1) "Cyclops" is the name of the group of giants, not of a particular one; 2) Cyclops have one eye, not two; 3) the Cyclops were mythical, not real: 4) plastic didn't exist when the Cyclops were supposed to have existed, and for that matter, 5) neither did glasses. The fraud was so easy to see through that Nicholas was sure even Davy wouldn't have fallen for it. And he was glad to discover that Sarah had also seen through it, and had just been pulling Travis's leg.

TAKING A TRIP (pp. 59–62)

The young man said he saw Gator run at his feet. But the young man could barely see without his glasses on, and his glasses weren't on at the time, because he was polishing them. He couldn't have recognized Gator. He also didn't see the sidewalk curb, which he tripped over.

PIECES OF PIZZA (pp. 65–67)

They cut the pizza into twelve slices. If Davy wanted pizza, they each got three slices. If he didn't, they each got four slices. Either way, the pieces were just the right size.

KIDNAPPED (pp. 69–72)

Ellie said she would often take the Bensons their newspaper and mail. If something had happened to the

Bensons, their newspaper and mail would have piled up. But there was nothing in the mailbox or on the porch. And, as Gator discovered, the other neighbors *had* been receiving their newspaper. Nicholas realized that the Bensons had probably just gone on vacation and put their newspaper and mail on hold.

VANDALISM! (pp. 75–78)

He showed Sarah that from inside the store, looking out through the window, the mysterious words now made sense:

MIAMI
HAWAII
TAHITI

They were in a travel agency, and the gang threat now became fantastic vacation getaways. "Humph," Sarah said. "They shouldn't be confusing us when we walk by like that. What's this town coming to?"

THE ELECTRIC GHOST (pp. 81–83)

The ghost appeared after the computer had been sitting unused during dinner, and disappeared when Gator hit a key. The ghost was a screensaver, a joke created by Alan.

FAST! EEE! THE SNOWMAN! (pp. 85–88)

Joseph had built his snowman on top of the car. But his mom had had errands to run. The hedge hid the car, but not the happy, traveling, snowman.

EGG-ZACTLY (pp. 89-92)

Sarah just reached into the water and pulled out an egg. But if the water had been boiling, Sarah would have seriously burned herself. She was just fine though, because the water wasn't boiling. It wasn't even hot. Sarah had put the pan on the stove, but had forgotten to turn on the burner. The egg was still raw.

AN ICE SURPRISE (pp. 95-98)

In the middle of winter, there would be no reason for a garden hose to be in the middle of the garage floor. And Dad was putting the sprinkler head back on the wall when they'd walked in. Dad was the magic fairy. He'd set a sprinkler up near the bush to run overnight. As the water fell on the bush through the night, it froze into an ice palace.

EARTHQUAKE! (pp. 101-103)

Sarah's glass of water had been filled to the top. When she took a drink after the shaking it was still filled to the top. If there had been an earthquake, the whole room would have shook, including the end table and the glass, and at least some of the water would have spilled out of the glass. Really, Sarah thought, an earthquake that could knock over a chair would probably have knocked over the whole glass. Yet, when she took a drink, the glass was full to the brim. She figured out quickly that Nicholas had knocked her stuff on the floor, shaken her bed, and then run to the light and pretended that he had just come into the room.

THE THIEF IN THE SHADOW (pp. 105–109)

They should look right in front of them. When Nicholas and Sarah entered the courtyard, the late afternoon sun was facing the statue, casting a shadow behind it. In the morning the statue's shadow would have been in front of it, not behind it as Jack had stated. Jack had not seen the thief, unless he had looked in the mirror.

TREED (pp. 111–114)

This time Joseph stood on Nicholas's shoulders. Joseph's long arms, which were several inches longer than Nicholas's, were just long enough to reach Porky.

SUNDAY FUNNIES (pp. 117–119)

If Sunday is the first day of the month, there will only be four Saturdays in April. Sarah had fallen for the newspaper's April Fools' Day prank.

WHERE'S DAVY? (pp. 121–124)

Gator.

RIDE 'EM GRANDPA (pp. 127–130)

Nicholas had read on the sign that the Pony Express only lasted for 18 months, from April 1860 to October 1861. Grandpa's grandpa couldn't have ridden with it for 20 years. And trains put the Pony Express out of business long before cars came on the scene.

NOT SO CLEAN GETAWAY (pp. 133–136)

The man said he'd been gardening all day. But a man who'd been gardening all day wouldn't be wearing clean boots and clean gloves.